My Year of Stories

By Abigail Shepherd

Published by Spud and Tufty-head Publishing.

Copyright © Abigail Shepherd 2017. All rights reserved. This book or any portion thereof may not be reproduced without permission from the author, except for the use of quotations in a book review.

For everyone at Bookmark, Congratulations on winning my Twitter competition! I hope you enjoy the book.

yours,
Abigail Shepherd

Contents

3. *January-* The Dandelion Clock
7. *February-* Walk
12. *March-* Mrs Drew
19. *April-* One Moment
23. *May-* Missing Mum
32. *June-* A Walk by the River
36. *July-* A New Life
47. *August-* One Little Act
49. *September-* Waiting
54. *October-* Pebbles
56. *November-* The Honeymooners
58. *December-* Mr West's Visit
71. *Acknowledgements*

January 2016

Am informed by hubby early this morning that I have An Email. Respond with studied casualness 'is it another "thanks but no thanks"?' He says actually it's a magazine agreeing to feature unpretentious short story I sent them without much hope. Wild ecstasy on my part follows. I re-download the app that will allow me to read said magazine, which I had deleted in a fit of despondency the day before.

'The Dandelion Clock' first appeared in Whim online magazine in February 2016 and was the first of my short stories to be accepted for publication.

The Dandelion Clock

"I am the most beautiful of all the flowers." The rose made this assertion with no self-consciousness. But the lily shook her delicate head.

"None is so elegant as the lily," she argued.

"The daffodil is the first sign of Spring. What can be more beautiful than a flower that stands for renewal?"

"You are all too obvious for true beauty," said the daisy. "Whereas I have a subtle prettiness that grows on you."

"I'm not only beautiful, but am cultivated all over the world for my special properties," preened the poppy.

"But you are all so common," interrupted the orchid. "I am both beautiful and rare."

The dandelion sighed. She was not where the others talked, but just outside. "I think you're all beautiful in your own ways."

The flowers nodded condescendingly. "Perhaps you're right. You at least have some perspective, for you certainly are not." They all tittered.

"No," replied the dandelion. "I'm not very pretty. But I have much to give if only others would see it. My leaves make a lovely salad, my stem can be sautéed and eaten, my root can be roasted and ground as a substitute for coffee, and even my flower is edible. But not many know these things and I'm not fashionable, though children sometimes enjoy blowing my seeds out for me."

"It must be horrible to be so overlooked," shuddered a stately iris.

"In some ways," answered the dandelion. "But not completely. For instance, that is why I'm out here, growing freely in the field. But you! I am sorry for you all."

"Why?"

The dandelion looked round at the marquee in which the other flowers blossomed. "Because of your beauty, you've been picked- to grace people's homes. But not for very long. Didn't you know? Picked flowers always die..."

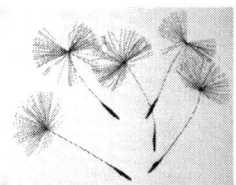

February 2016

Send another two short stories out to seek their fortunes. One I'm really happy with and feel convinced is of Great Literary Merit. The other I'm just making use of because I have written it and might as well give it a go. Have no doubt at all that the latter will be successful and work of Great Literary Merit will vanish into oblivion.

Turns out I was correct in this assumption as I have just had an email to say that 'Walk' has been published. No word from prospective publishers of story of Great Literary Merit.

'Walk' first appeared in Pulchritude Press in February 2016.

Walk

"Just keep putting one foot in front of the other," I told myself, glancing at the unrelenting back in front of me. It seemed we'd been walking for days, and the landscape that had thrilled me at first dwindled into sucking peat between tufts of heather under my boots. My companion was undaunted by the treacherous ground, leaping easily from tuft to tuft. He didn't look back to see if I followed. He knew I would. What choice did I have?

    The blisters were almost unbearable, but there was no way to stop. I'd long decided that this was a Death March. It just couldn't get any worse. Then the snow started. The figure ahead stopped and looked back. I straightened. He came towards me and I forced myself to look unconcerned.

    "I'd hoped to get a bit further, but we'd better head to the nearest shelter."

    "Fine. Where is it?"

"Only a couple of miles."
"A cou... I mean, okay. Whatever."
"Let's go. We'll have to move fast."

I'd been under the impression that we were already going fast, but soon realised I'd been mistaken. When he saw I couldn't keep up he grabbed my hand and practically dragged me. After the first mile we could no longer see where we were headed and he was relying entirely on his compass. My eyes went dizzy and I lost all sense of direction and time. The only thing I still felt was the numbing coldness on my face and in my mind.

"We're here."

I looked up to see a rough stone hut with the door tied shut by a bit of rope. We pulled it loose and stumbled in. It was such a relief to be out of the blizzard but, in truth, the bothy offered very little by way of comfort. The floor was stone, wooden benches lined the walls, doubling as tables and beds. Every visitor had left their name scratched on them, or drawn on the walls and rafters. But there was a log burner at one end and I saw there was a pile of wood, some matches, and a packet of fire-lighters beside it.

"You get the fire started, I'll look for some more stuff to burn," he barked at me, then disappeared. I yanked off my gloves and knelt to the fire. My hands trembled with cold and for a while it seemed impossible that my fingers would grasp a match. Then I thought what he, the Sergeant Major as I'd now designated him, would say if he came back and I hadn't lit the fire. Fear gave me the impetus I needed. I struck it and even that small yellow flame seemed to make everything warmer. I touched it to the fire-lighters I'd put in the grate, then flung some twigs on it. It went up with a whoosh.

When he came back with more wood I was replacing my boots after sorting my blisters. I looked at the wood. "It's soaked."

"I got them out of the peat bog. No trees round here if you hadn't noticed. Stack them so they can dry by the fire."

I almost saluted but resisted the urge. Once I'd stacked them and then watched him get a little kettle from his rucksack, fill it with water and place it on the stove, I was even able to smile.

We kept feeding the fire until the room warmed and we were able to take off our wet coats and hang them on the rafters to dry. Then the kettle boiled and two sachets of powdered chocolate appeared. By the time the magic rucksack had also produced a packet of biscuits to eat I was exhilarated by the experience and remembering why I was with this man. Then he turned to me. "This wasn't what I wanted our first walk to be like. I'm sorry if I snapped at you. But it could've been a disaster."

"I understand."

He grinned. "It's quite an adventure, isn't it?"

"Yes, it is."

"I expect it's put you off hillwalking though?"

I thought about it. "You know what? I love it!"

March 2016

Hopping up and down with impatience to hear from various competitions I've entered, knowing full well that there isn't the smallest chance of hearing anything for at least a month. Really should go back to first draft of novel but tell myself that I'm building a portfolio to impress an agent. Since I've had no luck finding one so far this seems as good an option as any.

'Mrs Drew' was shortlisted for the Soundwork UK short story competition and has since appeared on my blog.

Mrs Drew

I took a long breath, squared my shoulders and marched into the office block.

"I'm here to see Gareth Drew."

The receptionist deigned to raise his eyes from his phone screen. "Yes ma'am. And you are?"

"I'm Mrs. Drew."

He looked hard at me. "Are you indeed?"

"Yes. So, can I see him? Now?"

"Well, the odd thing is, ma'am, that I just showed Mrs. Drew upstairs twenty minutes ago."

I stared. "Are you suggesting my husband's a bigamist? Don't be silly."

"Well, it's either that, ma'am, or one of you is not Mrs. Drew."

"Then who is this other woman?"

"Mrs. Drew, according to her."

"Yes, but she's clearly not, because I am."

He was silent.

"Don't you believe me?" My voice was rising.

"It's just that she was here first, you see. It makes her more credible."

"Nonsense. It's the other way round. If you know you're making a false claim and the person you're pretending to be is likely to turn up, you'd make damn sure you were first. If you didn't know, then you'd be second."

"If you say so, ma'am."

"Oh, this is ridiculous! Get my husband down here at once. He will be able to identify me."

"Mr. Drew is not here, ma'am."

"Not here? Why not?"

"That's the other funny thing. Mr. Drew resigned yesterday. The other Mrs. Drew, she knew. She's up there getting his things."

"Whoever she is, she has no right to his things! I see it all now. This is an elaborate plan to steal something he has! Call her down!"

"Ma'am..."

"I insist you call her down. Or I shall phone the police."

He sighed. "One moment."

Ten minutes later the lift opposite me pinged. The doors slid open like curtains on a stage. "Veronica!" I exclaimed. The impeccably turned out blonde raised an eyebrow.

"Heidi? What are you doing here? I haven't seen you since college."

I laughed. "And how long ago it seems. What are you doing here?"

The receptionist coughed. I expect he meant to be discreet. "This is Mrs. Drew, ma'am."

"So you finally admit it," I sighed.

"I mean that this lady is Mrs. Drew."

"Veronica? Veronica isn't Mrs. Drew. She's Veronica Blake. An old friend from college."

"Don't you remember that I married Gareth?" asked Veronica. I recoiled.

"You're not married to Gareth. You're not Mrs. Drew. I did. I am."

"Heidi? What are you talking about? You came to our wedding."

"No. No! You came to our wedding. Why are you doing this? Is this some kind of joke?"

Veronica turned to the receptionist. "She's always been obsessed with my husband."

"Where's Gareth? I want to see him!"

"I'll call him." The cow even had my husband on speed dial. "Maybe you need to hear this from him."

Veronica walked away and the receptionist and I were left avoiding one another's eyes. I went over to an abstract metal chair and sat, drumming my fingers on the polished surface. At length, Veronica came back.

"He's coming over."

By now, I had an inkling that this wasn't to go my way. Veronica evidently had an understanding with Gareth. I guessed I no longer needed to demand the identity of the blonde I'd seen him with yesterday. Was she going to steal my life? Tomorrow morning would it be she who made Gareth his sandwiches and kissed him goodbye at the door? Would she be waiting to share dinner and wine with him when he got home? Would it be her who spent the day vacuuming dog hairs from our cream carpet and unnecessarily watering cacti? Was that what he wanted?

When Gareth walked in I knew it was true. He looked right past me, as though we hadn't just shared five years of our lives, his gaze resting on Veronica. "What's going on?"

Veronica gestured in my direction. "It's Heidi. You remember? From college? She thinks she's married to you."

"What?"

"I am," I choked. "You may choose to deny it, but it will still be the truth."

"Heidi, I had no idea…"

"Oh, stop. I don't want to hear any more lies."

He and Veronica exchanged a glance. "This has gone way too far," said Gareth, coming over to me. I thought he was going to say it was okay. That it had all been a big joke. A game. But he said, "I think you need professional help." And, looking from one to the other, I knew there was no escape.

"So that's how I ended up here."

"And how does that make you feel?" my psychiatrist asks, pen poised.

"Like everything I knew was a lie."

"Yes. Ye-es. Now the question is, Heidi, was it Gareth and Veronica who lied to you? Or your own mind?"

I pause. I know what she wants me to say. And I so badly want to get my life back.

"Heidi?"

"My own mind," I say.

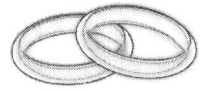

April 2016

Have had another story accepted for publication. Feel like I'm on my way to being a 'real writer'. Would like to make some money next time though. Spend an unprofitable half hour imagining the day when, as a successful author, I meet certain current customers at unspecified social function and can point out to them that just because someone does manual labour for a living does not mean they are of inferior intelligence. Remind myself that I should be writing, otherwise this will never happen. Drink tea instead.

'One Moment' first appeared in Platform For Prose.

One Moment

I was not in an even slightly romantic mood. I'd had an enormous row with my husband just moments ago and tonight's dinner was getting thrown into the trolley any old how. I almost wanted something to break. Only that would involve talking and explanations and apologising, and I wasn't in the mood for that either. A headache was brewing behind my eyes and I just wanted to get home, eat, and forget about the whole disaster of a day.

The people around me were irritating; why couldn't they just shop somewhere else? Especially whoever that was, with his big boots just where I wanted to go. I stopped and looked up. And up. The guy was well over six foot, not much older than me, with a bushy beard. Not my type at all. And yet, as our eyes met, the oddest flash passed between us. It wasn't just physical attraction. As I said, he wasn't my type, and I knew I wasn't looking my best with my red face and stony expression. No, it was more like a connection. Like we recognised each other without ever having met. But it was so quick, so transient, and I'd already walked away. But I knew that wouldn't be the end.

Sure enough, as I stood trying to remember what else was on my list, he came and stood next to me. We were at the end of an aisle, he couldn't be looking at something else. He was just standing close. I knew what to do. I should look up, smile, address a remark to him. Just something commonplace. He would understand. But I couldn't think of anything to say. And did I want to? Really? I touched my wedding ring. Yes, we'd had an argument, but was that a good enough reason to throw our marriage away because of one look? It might not be any better. I didn't believe in soulmates. So I did nothing and he walked away.

I saw him one more time, after I'd rejoined my husband at the checkout. He came up behind us in the queue.

I'd have smiled, but he didn't look at me. The relief and disappointment were equal.

"Let's go home, shall we?" asked my husband. That was his way of apologising. He never said sorry, just pretended nothing had happened.

"Okay," I said. We took a bag each and walked out together. I looked back once, but he'd gone.

May 2016

Celebration is indicated- have actually sold a story. Not simply managed to induce a publication to let me foist It on them, but have actually received coinage for it. Granted, payment is in Canadian dollars and by the time exchange rate and fees have been accounted for it amounts to around £3.00. But pleasure is nevertheless undimmed and have bought charming little notebook with the proceeds.

'Missing Mum' was first published in Mystery Weekly Magazine.

Missing Mum

One year after it happened, we all travelled back to Scotland. An eight hour journey, accomplished in almost complete silence. We each had too many thoughts we couldn't share and some we didn't want to admit, even to ourselves.

Luke, my boyfriend, stretched beside me. He hadn't known Mum, he was just here for support. Dad was driving. He hadn't been the same since. But it's my brother, Carl, who'd taken it hardest. He'd not been able to get over the fact that their last words to each other were angry ones. We'd all argued with her that day, though. And the day before. I guess it had become a habit, especially between her and Dad. I would always remember the end of their last one...

"I'm tired of being treated like I'm of no importance. I'm not your servant, I'm your wife!"

"And don't I know it. Nag, nag, nag..."

"I wouldn't nag if you showed some appreciation."

"Maybe I would show some appreciation if you didn't nag."

And then the capitulation and the fatal words... "Whatever. I'm going for a walk."

Mum never came back from that walk.

"We're here."

'Here' was the little log cabin we'd been holidaying in. And, up on that hill somewhere, was Mum. Sometimes I pictured her, lying with a broken leg, shouting for help. We'd searched for weeks, but we never found her. Carl thought she must have fallen into a peat bog. I could see her, sinking lower and lower, unable to get out, getting icy cold and knowing there was no chance of rescue, because we didn't know where she was. But those images were preferable to the other ones. I shook my head to clear it.

Everyone was turning to look at me, still sat in the car. "Come on, Mandy."

"Sorry," I said, scrambling out and taking a deep breath of chilly, thin air.

Luke came over and took my bag. "What's wrong?"

"I was just remembering."

"Your mum?"

"Yes. Wishing she and Dad hadn't argued." We hurried into the cabin, which had the musty smell of little use. Dad already had the kettle on. Carl favoured the stronger refreshment from his hip flask. I flicked the switch on the gas fire and we huddled on a sofa nearby. The tartan blanket thrown over it felt damp.

"That wasn't the only argument your mum had that day though, was it?" murmured Luke.

"How do you know that?"

"Carl told me."

"Yes. He had a massive row with her too."

"What about?"

"He'd just come in from outside and asked her to come downstairs and fetch his snowboard up. Which she didn't mind. She was good like that. But she minded when Carl came up the stairs right behind her, empty handed. I'd never seen her so mad."

"I don't blame her. Why did he do that?"

We paused as Dad came over and handed us each a scalding mug. I only answered when he'd gone again. I didn't know why.

"He said she wasn't doing anything important, and he was."

"'Pretty selfish.'"

"Yeah," I said, blowing on my tea. "She said she'd never help such an ungrateful brat again."

"I didn't know about all that. The row Carl told me about was the one you had with her."

"Oh. That."

"Is it true she was going to start charging you rent if you didn't start helping her round the house?"

I nodded. I felt bad about that.

"Sounds like you all took her for-granted."

"We did. And she tried so hard to get through to us and she never could."

"Why not?"

"Oh, I don't know. Dad always treated her outbursts like they were of no importance. So I s'pose we did too."

"He's not seeing anyone else? Your dad?"

"No. I think he thought about it. But it's harder than he imagined it would be."

Carl approached our corner. "Dad thinks we should go now or it will be too late." We had to do it that evening since we were driving back home again the next day. None of us had wanted to stay longer.

Carl cast a sideways look at my boyfriend. "Did Mandy tell you we're going up the hill to where she was last seen?"

"Yes. We're letting off Chinese lanterns, right? It's a nice idea."

"It's all that's left to us, since they never found her body."

"It must be hard not knowing what happened to her."

"Hard? It's unbearable!" blurted Carl, turning on his heal. We both followed him with our eyes. "It's been really tough on him," I said, rising from the sofa.

"Tough on you all."

"Yes. But his last words to her were that he wished she was dead."

"Ah."

"Yes. The police had a ball with that."

"Well, it does sound suspicious."

"Carl isn't capable of violence." But he was capable of negligence, I thought. I could see him being so angry with Mum that he deliberately ignored her when we went out to search. He might have pretended he hadn't seen her and walked right by. Regretted it when he was calm; too late. But of course, that was nonsense. A figment of overwrought imagination.

I took my unfinished tea through to the kitchen and poured it away, watching till the last dregs had disappeared down the drain.

"Let's go, shall we?"

Dad and Carl got back in the front of the Land-rover and Luke and I clambered into the back. It was a short drive up the hill but we had to go slowly, thanks to the dusting of snow on the ground. It was much like it had been a year ago and I shivered. Mum wouldn't have lasted long in this.

"Have you got the Chinese lanterns?" I asked Dad.

"Of course," he snapped. I started. It was the same tone he used to use to Mum. I think he realised it too. "Sorry, Mandy. I'm just a bit het up."

I nodded but found myself staring at the back of Dad's head. A horror movie of him following her outside and creeping up behind her was playing in my mind. I turned away. It must have been an accident. Couldn't have been anything else. But if only I knew. I just hoped that, whatever had happened, she hadn't died thinking we didn't love her, even if we were a bit selfish about it.

The Land-rover stopped at the side of a hill loch. A car had passed by this spot last year and the occupants had seen Mum, standing right here, staring at the choppy water. As though she was waiting for something. It seemed like I saw her there now; a lone figure in jeans and a raincoat. In a moment she would fill her pockets with rocks and head purposefully into the water. And that was the worst image of all because I shared a burden of that guilt.

We got out the car. I blinked a few times. The figure hadn't moved. What if I wasn't imagining it? Every pulse in my body was thumping. What if?

"Hello darlings. Did you miss me?"

June 2016

It is a source of unfailing satisfaction to me when one of my stories or articles, previously rejected by an editor unable to recognise my genius, is released on my blog to vociferous applause. Editors don't know everything.

'A Walk by the River' was written (and rejected) in the first half of 2016, but proved extremely popular when later published on my blog.

A Walk by the River

"So, you and your husband had gone for a walk?"

"Yes," I confirmed, repressing a sigh. The glaring lights were giving me a headache. "Do we have to go over all this again? You have my original statement."

"Indeed. In it you say that your husband slipped and fell into the river."

"Yes." I stared at the table. The laminate was cracked and I tried peeling a piece off. It needed a good clean. "I tried to help him, but the current was too strong."

The detective nodded. "However, there was a large injury on the back of his head."

"Not surprising when he'd been bashed about in the water!"

"No." He was circling round something, but I wasn't sure what. "The surprise is, though, that the blow on his head was what killed him. He didn't drown."

There was a pause. I didn't know what I was expected to answer. I noticed in a detached way that my manicure was chipped and scratched from scrabbling around at the edge of the river, trying to reach him and knowing I couldn't, calling for help and knowing there was none.

"There was almost no water in his lungs. He was dead before he went into the water." He paused and leaned forward, lowering his voice. "You know what I think?"

I shook my head, feeling an absurd desire to giggle. The same sort of feeling I had at funerals or when my passport was being checked at an airport. Surely he didn't believe I'd done anything?

"I think you hit him harder than you intended."

I thought back to that sickening moment when my husband fell and forced myself to breathe normally. "No."

"He'd betrayed you," he continued. "You were angry and you didn't hold back enough."

"I keep telling you, I didn't know about his gambling addiction."

"That's what you say. But you found out, didn't you? And so you suggested a walk and murdered him."

"A bit melodramatic. Divorce might have been a better option."

"Perhaps. Only you'd have got no money that way. He'd gambled everything away, even remortgaged your house."

"Killing him wouldn't get my home back," I answered, closing my eyes on the word 'home'. Twenty years I'd spent, getting it just right, and now...

"The life insurance should help."

"I sure hope so."

He shuffled his papers, then looked back up, saying, "you know, if you'd just stunned him, it would have been the perfect crime."

I licked my lips, tasting blood red lipstick. "You can't prove it."

July 2016

Have finally heard back from competition entered in February. Short story has been selected to receive a commendation. Am now very glad I accepted invitation to award ceremony.

Award ceremony turns out interesting. Attend writing workshop first, which is enlivened by presence of individual who seems to think we are there to hear him talk, rather than celebrated author. Ceremony itself is very long and am grateful that I am commended, not shortlisted, as said unfortunates have to read their stories out loud. This takes two hours and press photographer doesn't bother to wait.

'A New Life' was commended in the William Soutar Writing Prize 2016 and published in a commemorative eBook by the AK Bell Library.

A New Life

I sometimes wondered what the waitress thought of me. A middle-aged woman who'd appeared out of the blue, coming in for coffee at the same time every day. She was certainly intrigued. Did she imagine a secret assignation? Or a rash promise? She served me with her eyes full of questions. I never enlightened her but, as the season changed from winter to spring, a rapport was built between us. I learned, I'm not sure how, that she was new here too. She didn't know it, but she was a far more interesting character. So young and pretty; her life should have been just starting. But that wasn't the impression she gave. At first, a few of the young workers coming in for bacon rolls would ask her out. She always said no. Eventually, they stopped. Except one. She had to admit to him that she was single, but went on saying no. In the end, I asked her about it.

"Why don't you go on a date with that nice boy who keeps inviting you?"

"I'm not thinking of romance. Can I get you anything else?"

"No, thank you. At least consider it?"

"I'm happy as I am."

"No, you're not."

"I beg your pardon?"

"You're not. I know you're not. I see myself reflected in you."

She nodded slowly. She'd seen it too. The overwhelming loneliness. "Happy enough, then," she said and walked away. Is anyone ever happy enough? Once I had been, but I didn't know it. And now it was gone. He was gone.

The next morning the girl finally screwed up her courage. Perhaps my personal question the day before made her feel she could.

"So, why do you come in here every day?"

"You'll wish you hadn't asked," I warned. "It's not at all romantic."

"Well?"

"It's because I have nothing better to do."

"Why not?"

I frowned. "What do you mean?"

"There's loads of stuff to do round here."

"I'm sure there is. But not... alone."

She sat down. "You don't have to be alone. This is such a great town. There's a walking club, a book club, a drama club and a quiz club. There's Pilate classes, Zumba classes and dancing classes. There's even pony trekking, white water rafting and fishing."

I put up my hand, laughing. "I think I'm a little old for some of those."

"You won't know if you don't try."

"All of this from a girl who won't even say yes to one date."

"That's different."

"Why?"

"I guess I've just lost faith in relationships," she shrugged, standing up. "I should get back to work."

She didn't speak to me again for two days, beyond bringing my coffee. Then on Wednesday she indicated towards a small group by the window. "That's the book club," she said. "They're always happy to take new members."

I sat and looked at the cheery gathering for some time. Then I sidled over and asked to join. They welcomed me with open arms.

"So you joined the book club, then?" said my waitress the next day.

"Seeing as how it was practically forced on me, yes."

"It'll be great fun. You'll see."

"So will a date."

"How do you know? Why are you recommending I go out with someone you don't even know anything about?"

"I know quite a bit about him, actually."

"Such as?"

"I know he always says please and thank you. Not just to you, but to the other waitress as well. I know he always speaks to you respectfully and that, when his eyes follow you round, it's your face he's looking at. I've heard him chatting on the phone to his mother. I've seen him pick up dropped things for elderly people. I've seen his reaction when his order has been wrong. I know he always smiles and says hello to a certain middle-aged lady who's always here at the same time. All these things tell me he's a nice guy."

She sighed. "I'm not looking for a boyfriend. I just got out an abusive relationship. I moved here to start again."

"So start again! Go on a date. The longer you wait, the harder it will be."

"I can't. I'm scared of it happening again."

"You know, there's lots of good relationships out there. I was married for thirty years. I won't say we never had a cross word. We did. Sometimes we said hurtful things that we didn't mean. But we both respected each other too much to let that degenerate into abuse."

"How did he die?"

"Heart attack. Six months ago. It was sudden."

"I'm sorry."

"Thanks. You'd better go and serve those people giving you dirty looks."

"Whoops. So I had."

She scurried off and I was left alone with my thoughts. But not for long.

"May I sit here? All the tables are taken."

I looked up to see a well turned out woman of about my own age.

"Of course," I said and she pulled out the chair opposite and slid gracefully into it.

"Thanks. The waitress didn't think you'd mind. I'm Marcia."

"Georgie. Nice to meet you."

"Are you on holiday?"

"No. I moved here about six months ago. Took early retirement."

"I've sometimes thought of that. But I guess I just like my job."

"What do you do?"

"I run gym classes. Zumba, Pilates, that sort of thing."

I shot my waitress a suspicious look but she was clearing tables with an air of aggressive innocence. "I see."

"You should join. It's great for ladies our age. Keeps us limber."

"I'll think about it."

"Great. Here's my card."

The next day I rang up and booked a course of Zumba classes. Then I went to the coffee shop as usual and told my waitress.

"That's great," she said. "Here's your latte. Have you ever thought of coming in one evening?"

"No, I haven't. Why would I?"

"Well, tonight is curry night and it's good fun."

"Is it some sort of club?" I sighed.

"No," said the waitress. "It's just a thing we do. Curry on a Friday night. There's always a great atmosphere."

"I'll think about it."

I did. After all, what harm could it do? It had to be better than a solitary boiled egg in a house that felt too empty to be home. In the end I dug out a sparkly jumper and went for it.

I'd expected to eat alone, but Marcia, my new Zumba instructor, and another woman I vaguely recognised from the book group waved me over.

"Come and sit with us. We can get to know each other."

I sat. Marcia, bless her, noticed the slightly puzzled glance I threw her companion. "Georgie, you've met Tess, haven't you?"

"Yes, of course. From the book group," I smiled. This hurdle over, we were chatting happily by the time the waitress came to take our order. She gave me a knowing smile, which I ignored. But it wasn't just about the curry night I realised, once we'd finished eating.

"We have to be going now," Tess told me. "It's quiz evening at the pub and we're both members of a team. Hey, you should come! We need all the help we can get."

Since this was endorsed by Marcia I went.

Two weeks later I didn't always sit alone to have coffee. On Wednesdays I sat with the book group. On Thursdays Marcia joined me after Zumba. Fridays I sat with Tess and a few others from the quiz team, swotting up on general knowledge. On Sundays I didn't go at all. I was busy learning to play golf. On my own initiative this time. And, though I would never forget my husband, I felt I was forging something new to live for. Something for myself. And the more that was true, the more I hated seeing a young girl too afraid to live.

"I want to thank you for everything you've done," I told her. "Will you come to my house for dinner one evening? Say, Saturday?"

"There's no need..."

"I know. I really want to."

"Okay."

She arrived promptly at six and I handed her a glass of wine. "I just have to see to the gravy. Go through to the living room. There's some company in there for you."

She frowned. "Company?"

"Yes. I figured you've done enough interfering in my life, so now I've interfered in yours."

"What have you done?"

"I've invited that nice boy round for dinner too."

"Georgie, no! I've told you. That's all at an end for me."

"You know what you've taught me over the past few weeks? There are no endings. Only new beginnings."

She sighed. "Fine. I'll go talk to him. I'll even be nice. But I'm making no promises."

She did though. She promised she would marry him. Then she promised to be with him till death. And now they've made a new life of their own. She'll be born in the spring and they're calling her Georgie.

August 2016

Must confess that I'm finding it a little difficult to get back to normal after all the excitement of award ceremony. It seems just one day of being recognised as an author in the 'real world' is enough to make me wish it a more regular occurrence. Except that I unhappily lack the courage to mention it in the 'real world.' My online writing world, on the other hand, is going swimmingly, with my blog and Instagram both going surprisingly well. I even come over as quite creditable.

Also, have had full manuscript request from a publisher. Am trying not to get hopes up, but...

'One Little Act' was written for a competition during this period, then later published on my blog

One Little Act

I started as someone pushed impatiently past, knocking their wire basket against my hip. Oh dear. They'd probably been tutting behind me for ages and I hadn't heard. I adjusted my hearing-aid and squinted at the rows of pet food. The cheaper cans were on the top shelf. They would be. I raised a stiff arm towards them.

"Can I help you?" said a voice. "Is this what you want?"

A young man deposited two tins of cat food into my trolley and went on his way. And I smiled the whole walk home.

September 2016

Have succeeded in selling another short story for actual money. The amount is still around the £3.00 mark and cannot but wonder if I have reached some kind of natural ceiling. Feel sure such was not the case for the likes of Hemmingway and Poe. Hope novel will earn slightly more when it releases.

'Waiting' was accepted for publication by The Flash Fiction Press in September 2016 and appeared on their website in the October.

Waiting

I've never seen a dead body before now. It isn't all that bad. I don't have to shake or poke her to make sure. She's just slumped in the bed, her skin paper white. The worst part is I'm not sure what to do. Do I call 999? It's not exactly an emergency. I mean, she's not going anywhere. I phone the emergency services anyway and they tell me to wait for an ambulance and the police to arrive. Why the police? It's clearly natural causes. But I do as I'm told and sit down in Effie's earthy living room to wait.

   At least she's not suffering anymore, I think. But it's sad she's been found by her home-help. She had no family. I've always pitied her for that. I can't wait for my Prince Charming to come and sweep me off my feet and give me lots of cute babies. Well, I'm in my early thirties now, so I suppose I've actually been waiting a while. It hadn't ever happened for Effie. She'd been all alone and now she was dead.

The cottage is a rural one, so I know the ambulance could take some time. When Effie was admitted to hospital a few months ago she'd complained it took half an hour to arrive.

"Disgraceful," she'd said. "I could've died. They should have sent the helicopter." It was a big thing among Effie's friends to have the air ambulance out to them. They'd get bragging rights for months- if they came back.

"Maybe next time," I'd answered. "Now, have you taken all your pills for today?" And she'd said she had, so I'd ticked that off the list and moved on to the next item. Effie could chat for ages but I'd always tried to keep it brief, otherwise I'd be late for my next client. Well, I'd be late today for sure.

Turns out it's a bit eerie being all alone with a dead body. Too quiet. I feel the need to do something normal, something that makes noise. I head to the kitchen to brew a coffee. I'd often done so whilst I fixed her a sandwich or a piece of toast. Funny, this is the last time the chipped mug and white plastic kettle will ever be used. I look round while it boils. On the table is Effie's scrapbook. These last few weeks of being completely housebound she'd amused herself by pasting all her old photos into a book. I turn a few leaves. They're nearly all pictures of Effie with her three best friends. It seems they used to get together for Bridge every week. And here's one of them at Bingo. Now an OAP lunch. A party. I smile at their narrow little lives. But they seem happy enough.

   The next page is a little different. Is that a luxury liner? I didn't know they'd been on a cruise. Around the Mediterranean by the looks of it. And here's another. Up the Nile this time. There's a picture of Effie in the Valley of the Kings. There are about six different cruises in all. I'm glad they had some fun.

   I turn a few more pages and here's Effie and her friends standing outside the Eiffel Tower... And the Taj Mahal... And The Leaning Tower of Pisa. And now they're taking a hot air balloon ride, white water rafting, skiing. In the minimal gaps between the photos are pasted tickets to various famous shows and attractions.

   I can't believe the old lady in that bed did so much. I no longer pity her. No wonder she never had a family, she was too busy having fun. Maybe she would have liked one, but she never let its absence stop her from living a great life. No wonder she'd chosen to spend her final weeks looking back over her past. She had some amazing memories.

   And I start thinking. Maybe next time I have a holiday I'll go somewhere. Egypt perhaps. Stop waiting for my Mr Darcy to come along and do something exciting. And maybe he'll come one day and maybe he won't, but it won't matter; I'll have lived a full life anyway. Like Effie did.

October 2016

Took a holiday this month, but would seem that you can't really take a holiday from writing. Had flash of inspiration while sauntering along beach and for once was actually able to write it down before becoming distracted and forgetting it forever.

'Pebbles' was published on my blog in October 2016 and was immediately extremely popular with the most comments I'd ever had, all complimentary.

Pebbles

The beach was more rocks than sand. He picked his way over the pebbles, irritated when they rolled beneath him, making him unsteady. This sunset walk she'd insisted on was not exactly easy going.

He looked back, wondering what was taking her so long. She was stooping. At first he thought she'd fallen. Then he saw the glistening pebble in her hand. She added it to an already bulging pocket.

And he realised, while he's seen them merely as obstacles to be got over as quickly as possible, she'd seen them as individual things of beauty, to be studied as she went. Now he had grit in his shoes, and she had a pocketful of treasures.

November 2016

Have always been told the real work starts after you find a publisher for your novel. Am in the happy position of being able to report that this is Indeed True. I'm managing to write a little flash fiction, but most of my time is being spent re-reading my manuscript with my editor until we are both heartily sick of it, not to mention discussing the relative advantages of lettuces compared to carrots. Also manure versus fertiliser. I know. Scintillating.

'The Honeymooners' was first written for a 100 word story competition, but was eventually published by The Drabble in January 2017.

The Honeymooners

"Where's the BMW?"

"It was rented. I returned it as, now we're married, we can share your Audi."

The bride frowned. "Problem. I took the Audi back too."

"Then buy a car. You're rich, right?"

"Not exactly. What about you, Mr Hot-shot Businessman? You buy a car."

"I'm not buying anything. Actually, if I don't get some cash soon my business will go under."

"So you're not rich either? Maggie said you were."

"She said you had money."

They both considered Maggie, last seen waving off the two most heartless gold-diggers she'd ever encountered with the discarded bouquet.

December 2016

Book is due for publication imminently. Will not scruple to say that I Am Terrified. More so at the idea of people reading it than the possibility of no one doing so. However, quite realise that I have a certain responsibility to help try and prevent the latter happening. To that end I've begun putting together a Mailing List, which sounds more impressive than it is since it so far consists of a little over twenty people, almost half of them family. Have decided to offer to new subscribers a prequel short story to my novel in order to drum up enthusiasm. Cannot say so far if working or not.

'Mr West's Visit' was offered as a free short story to newsletter subscribers in the month of January. It did work.

Mr West's Visit

Vicky would never forget the day Mr West came to visit. It was a bitter January afternoon, too icy for school, and she and Mary-Anne were sat by the stove stroking some fluffy brown ducklings that would freeze outside. Ma was upstairs, teaching eight year old Lizzie to darn. Sally the maid was preparing supper. And Pa was in town, they thought. But then the door opened and he was there, stamping snow from his boots and letting in a whirl of coldness. And behind him was another man, a shadowy figure in a dark coat and hat.

"Come and warm your hands at the stove, Mr West," invited Pa.

"Thank you," said the man, shrugging off his coat and scattering icy droplets over the floor in the process. Sally gave them a dirty look. It would be her job to mop them up.

"These are two of my daughters, Victoria and Mary-Anne," continued Pa.

"A pleasure," Mr West bowed. Giggling, the two girls stood and curtsied.

"Mind the ducklings," warned Vicky as he seemed about to step on them.

"What an odd thing to have in the house, Mr Bloom!"

But Pa only smiled and said "Needs must, Mr West."

Ma came down at the sound of a strange voice. "Ah, there you are, Harriet," said Pa. "This is Mr West. He's in town on business, but they're all full up at the inn. I said he could stay here for a few days." There was a mixture of laughter and apprehension in Pa's eyes, but Ma behaved beautifully.

"You're very welcome, sir. Sally, lay another place for supper won't you? Vicky, can I have a quick word?"

Vicky got up and followed Ma out the room. "There's no time to get the guest room ready," Ma told her. "He'll have to sleep in your room and you can go in with Lizzie and Mary-Anne."

"But Ma, that's not fair! Why me? Why can't Charlie give up his room?"

"And go where? I'm sorry Vicky but this is the simplest solution. It will only be for a few days."

Vicky repeated these words to herself many times that evening. It's only for a few days, it's only for a few days. She did so when Mr West told Ma she'd overcooked the bacon. She did so when he asked for a different pudding and Ma had to open one of the precious jars of jam and make up a quick pastry, just so he could have a tart. She did so when he made a slighting reference to his room. "I'd no idea you didn't have a proper guest room, ma'am," he said. "I wouldn't have put you to the trouble if I had."

"There wasn't time to clean and air the guest room for you, Mr West," was all Ma said.

"Of course, of course. Forgive me. No doubt you will do so tomorrow."

So the next morning, Ma and Sally put aside their plans and prepared the guest room. Mr West did not offer to help with it, or with anything else. Pa and Charlie went off to work on the farm and left him ensconced by the parlour fire, reading Pa's newspaper and eating Ma's cake. He stayed there until after dinner, then yawned and said he would take a walk down to the town. He returned a few hours later, smelling of beer.

"You know what would go really well with this cheese?" he said at supper. "A nice bit of chutney. You do have some chutney, don't you ma'am? As excellent a housekeeper as yourself surely must do."

"Fetch the chutney from the pantry, please Vicky," said Pa. Vicky knew that there was only one jar of chutney left, and Ma was saving it for the special meal she'd planned for her and Pa's wedding anniversary in a few weeks. But she went into the back hall and retrieved the jar from the pantry, muttering under her breath as she did so.

When she got back, Mr West was talking about London.

"You've never seen anything like it," he was saying. "Wet streets glowing in gaslight, the smoke from a hundred factories, everyone busy, everyone with a place." He turned to Charlie. "A man can really make something of himself there."

Vicky thought it sounded horrible and she expected Charlie to scorn the idea. But he just nodded, with a funny look on his face. It looked, well, rapt. Pa gave Charlie a sharp glance and changed the subject.

Vicky was wakeful that night. She kept thinking about the look on Charlie's face. He was only fourteen, less than two years older than her. He couldn't want to go to London. Could he?

"Stop fidgeting," murmured Mary Anne, so she tried to keep still. But that just made it worse. In the end she got up, intending to fetch a glass of milk from the pitcher downstairs. She tiptoed past Pa and Ma's room so as not to wake them, but they were still up, talking in hoarse whispers.

"He has to go, Charles, he's eating us out of house and home. And I won't have him telling my children they should leave."

"I know. But tomorrow's the market. That's what he came for. I'm sure he'll go after that."

Mr West did come with them to the market. But when Ma had sold all the eggs and was ready to go home, he magically appeared and hopped back into the cart. Vicky asked him a few questions about what he'd been doing, but he wouldn't say much. He had no purchases and didn't seem to have gone to any stalls. She guessed he'd been at the Franton Arms again. He was up to something, she was sure.

At dinner, Pa asked if his business had gone well.

"Not as well as I'd hoped," he said.

"But it's nearly done?.

"I wouldn't say that."

"The Franton Arms will probably have some vacancies now the market is over. How about we go and see tomorrow?"

But Mr West was shaking his head. "Can't do business on a Sunday, my dear Mr Bloom. You know that."

Pa sighed, but said no more. Ma's lips were tightly pressed together.

"How about some wine, Mrs Bloom?" asked their guest. "I'm sure you have some?"

"I'm afraid our wine is only for medicinal use and special occasions," answered Ma.

"Is it, indeed?" he replied, seemingly amused. "I see."

"Tell us more about London," interrupted Charlie. Vicky couldn't bear it and stood up.

"I have a headache, Ma. May I go to bed?"

"Of course, dear," said Ma, looking as though she wished she could too.

Mr West accompanied them to church the next day. After the sermon, he was keen to talk to all their neighbours. "I'm staying with the Blooms," he would say. "Lovely place. Though they refuse to serve their guests any wine! Not that I'm complaining, of course. No doubt they have their reasons. I'm just such a generous person myself, it's hard to understand."

Vicky could feel Ma stiffening beside her. Luckily, Mr West didn't want to come back for dinner. "I'm engaged to a friend at the inn," he explained. "I'll see you at supper."

"He has to go," said Ma, on the way home. "Tomorrow."

"I like him," protested Charlie. The girls exchanged exasperated glances.

"He has no reason to stay longer," answered Pa.

But at supper, Mr West said, "You know, I think I'll stay till the next market. I can complete my business then."

"Certainly. I'm sure the inn will have room for you now," Pa replied.

"Yes, perhaps. I'll certainly go there if you can't afford to have me any longer. I'm sure your neighbours will understand. Not everyone does well at farming."

"I'm thinking only of your comfort, sir," Pa said through gritted teeth.

"Oh, I'm very comfortable here, thank you."

"Charles," Ma rose. "Can I have a word?"

Vicky desperately wanted to know what they were saying. She got up too, and went over to poke the range fire. It was right next to the door.

"I know, Harriet," Pa was saying. "But I'm trying to get the squire to invest in some new machinery for us. I can't have rumours going about that we aren't doing very well. It would ruin everything. It will only be for a few more days."

Vicky's mind was now made up. She had to do something. Just as well she'd had an idea.

The next day she followed Mr West when he again went to the village in the afternoon. As she expected, he headed for the Franton Arms. She couldn't go in without attracting a lot of attention, so she sneaked through the back door and tiptoed upstairs to a storeroom located just above the bar. If she lay down with her ear to the floorboards, she could hear what was said. There was even a crack big enough to look through. It was a pity she couldn't see and hear at the same time, but it couldn't be helped.

She spotted Mr West straight away. He was standing at the bar, holding a wad of money. She lowered her head to listen. "Drinks on me," he said, and a cheer went up.

"You're a right one, Mr West," said one man, whose voice Vicky knew as belonging to a farm labourer.

"Nonsense, lad," he answered. "You deserve it. Working for a pitiful wage, day in and day out, all for those ungrateful, rich idiots. They'd be nothing without you, just you remember that. In London, now..."

Vicky had heard enough. She scrabbled up and brushed the worst of the dust from her dress. Then she went boldly downstairs and entered the tap room. A hush descended.

"Mr West," said Vicky, borrowing from Ma, "could I have a word? In private."

Mr West followed her out to the hallway, looking slightly apprehensive. "Well, what is it?"

"I know why you're here now. You're recruiting farm labourers to work in a London factory."

"What of it?"

"Only that I think the squire and other farmers won't be too happy when I tell them. Nor will my pa. No one will blame him when he asks you to leave. To put it bluntly, you've outstayed your welcome and I want you to go."

"I should have known you hoity-toity lot wouldn't want a plain worker like me taking any of your profits. Not even a bottle of wine!"

"You're mistaken. We aren't wealthy. We don't begrudge hospitality, but you've eaten the last of our jam, the last of our chutney, and you would have had the last of our wine too if we'd let you. In fact, from what I can see," she glanced at the pocket where he'd stowed the money, "you're rather richer than we are. I think leaving some of that as a thank you would be a lovely gesture when you go this afternoon, don't you?"

Mr West spluttered a bit, but Vicky was firm and he saw there was nothing for it. He came back to the farm, packed his bag, and was gone.

   Pa and Ma never knew why he left so suddenly, but they couldn't disguise their relief. They were even more surprised that he left some money. Ma used it to buy some extra food from the village shop to replace what he'd eaten, and it was almost as if he'd never been there. Almost. Apart from the sullen and discontented way Charlie now went about his chores. He, for one, would never be the same again.

Acknowledgements

Many thanks to my market research team- Julia Blake, Nadia L King, Kelsey Stone, Diana Tyler, Ellen Read, V. P. Colombo, Soulla Christodoulou, Jenny Glover and Becky Wright. Your advice was invaluable and I couldn't have done it without you. Thanks must also go to all the editors who've said 'yes' to publishing my stories. And finally, thank you to you, the reader.

If you enjoyed this collection, please support the author by giving it a nice review.

Printed in Great Britain
by Amazon